This igloo book belongs to:

....

igloobooks

Published in 2017
by Igloo Books Ltd
Cottage Farm
Sywell
NN6 0BJ
www.igloobooks.com

HUN001 0717
2 4 6 8 10 9 7 5 3 1
ISBN 978-1-78670-306-4

Illustrated by Mark Chambers
Written by Melanie Joyce

Printed and manufactured in China

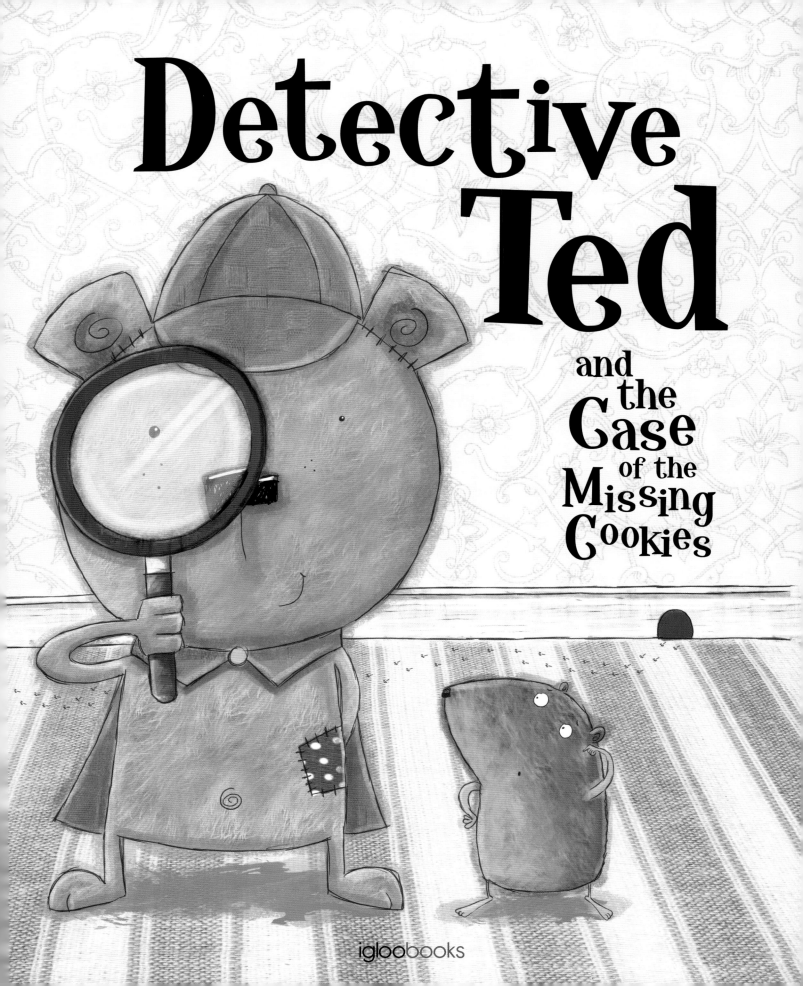

Detective Ted

and the Case of the Missing Cookies

igloobooks

DO NOT DISTURB!

There was a **mystery** at Edward's house.
At nighttime, someone was creeping about.
They chewed on cookies and nibbled at books.
They left holes in slippers and Edward's old socks.

The culprits came in the **dead** of **night**,
when everyone was tucked in tight.

"There's one thing to do," Edward said.
"I'll have to be **Detective Ted.**"

"I'd better hurry. There's not much time.
I must follow the clues and **solve** this crime."

... past the big
potted plant...

He followed a trail of cookie
crumbs that led along the floor...

... and the blue bathroom door.

Then, Ted saw a shape,
a shadow lurking in the hall.
It moved across the carpet...
... past the clock... along the wall.

It wasn't a thief or a burglar **at all.**
It was **Sid** the hamster, creeping down the hall.

"Help me, please,
Detective Ted," he said.
"Burglars have stolen my food
and all the straw from my bed!"

Then, at the bottom of the stairs,
there was rustling and giggling,
followed by pitter-patter noises
and long, pink tails wiggling.

Suddenly, the kitchen door closed with a click.
"**Come on,**" said Detective Ted.
"**We've got to catch them, quick.**"

Ted stood on a chair and opened the kitchen door.
"Come on, Sid," he said and he grabbed him by the paw.

There, in the kitchen,
were **three burglar rats**,
who had snuck in the back door
and tied up the cat.

The greedy rats **gobbled** all the jello and ice cream,
Then they rubbed their fat bellies and hatched a new scheme.

"We'll take all the swag," they said, "away to our nest.
Then we'll **sneak back in later** and steal the rest."

Suddenly, in the hallway,
there was a very loud **BONG!**
as the rattly, old clock
shook and struck one.

Everyone jumped, even the rats.
They looked around, startled and said,
"What was that?"

Suddenly Detective Ted slipped
and his wooden chair wobbled.
"Hold on!" he said to Sid,
but the chair rocked and toppled.

In the kitchen, Ted slid and landed with a splat,
right in the middle of the bad burglar rats.
"I'm Detective Ted!" he cried. "You're under arrest.
Hand over the loot and then clean up this mess."

The rats looked at each other.
Then, they looked back at Ted.
They **fell down laughing,**
and then they said,

"So, you think you're a detective?
You're not very cool...
... Don't mess with us, teddy,
you'll just look like a fool."

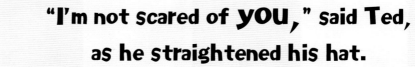

"I'm not scared of **YOU**," said Ted,
as he straightened his hat.

"You're stealing things that aren't yours.
You're **bad** burglar rats."

The rats stopped their laughing. They held up their paws.
Then they flashed their long teeth and their sharp, scratchy claws.

"Oh, dear," whispered Ted,
as he backed through the door.
The rats crept **toward** him.
Their shadows moved across the floor.

Then, something **strange** happened.
It was amazing and weird.
There was a **gurgling** sound
and a monster appeared.

It was covered in **bristles** and had a **big, feathery head.**
It rolled one **massive** eyeball, **lurched** forward and said,

"Urggh!"

"Argh!" shrieked the rats.
They dashed this way and that,
then they **darted** and **dived**
through the swinging cat flap.

They scrambled and scurried and ran up the path.
"**Good riddance!**" cried Ted, "and don't come back!"

Detective Ted smiled. **"Come out, Sid,"** he said.
Sid chuckled and shook the feather duster off his head.

**"Those rats were just cowards. They've run off. They've fled.
We make a great team, you and I,"** said **Sid** to Detective **Ted.**

There was a **mess** to clean up.
They had to work on.
Soon the morning would come
and the night would be gone.

So, they untied the cat
and turned off the lights.

Then, they all trudged upstairs
and said, **"Goodnight."**

Soon, Sid was snoring and so was the cat.
Edward took off his cloak and his old-fashioned hat.
Just for tonight, there would be **no more crime**.
That is, until Detective Ted was needed **next time!**

"Goodbye, see you soon!"